I Am
A BLACK GIRL

I Am
A BLACK GIRL

Written by Cindy Similien
Illustrated by Palwasha Sajid

ISBN: 9798625007566

To contact the author, please email:
CSJ Media Publishing
csjmediapublishing@gmail.com

This book is dedicated to Patience Heaven Albert, and every beautiful Black girl around the world – past, present, and future.

I know who I am.
There is no one quite like me.
I am unique - one of a kind.

I am a Black girl, and I am BRAVE.
I am ready to conquer the day
and everything that comes my way.

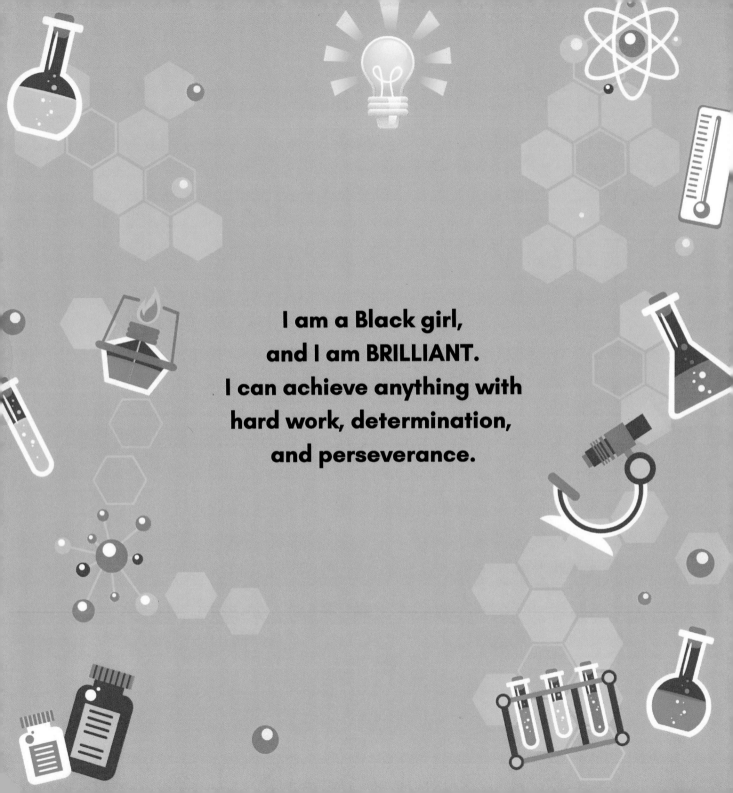

I am a Black girl,
and I am BRILLIANT.
I can achieve anything with
hard work, determination,
and perseverance.

I am a Black girl, and I am BOLD.
I shine my light wherever I go.

I am a Black girl, and I am BEAUTIFUL.
I love everything about me -
from the top of my head
all the way down to my toes.

I am a Black girl, and I am BELOVED.
I treat myself and others with
love, kindness, honor, and respect.

I am a Black girl, and I am the BEST.
I am my ancestors' wildest dream.

I am a Black girl, and I BELONG.
I am at the right place at the right time.
I make a difference in my community
and around the world.

I am a BLACK girl,
and I am:
Brave,
Brilliant,
Bold,
Beautiful,
Beloved,
the Best,
and I Belong.

The End.

About the Author

Cindy Similien is an award-winning Haitian-American author, cultural ambassador, and women & girls empowerment advocate. Her life's motto is: "Live to love; work to improve the lives of others; and create a legacy." She studied English Literature and Creative Writing at Barnard College-Columbia University.

Other Children's Books By Cindy Similien

Haiti Is

Ayiti Se
(Haitian Creole Edition)

Haití Es
(Spanish Edition)

Just A Kid With A Dream

Today, I Am Thankful For...

Mateo Goes to Cape Verde

Made in the USA
Monee, IL
21 February 2021

60905544R00017